Out of Sight

by Kitty Fross

Illustrated by Vince Deporter

Cover illustrated by A&J Studios

SCHOLASTIC INC.

New York Toronto London Auckland Sydney
Mexico City New Delhi Hong Kong Buenos Aires

Published by Scholastic Inc.,
90 Old Sherman Turnpike, Danbury, Connecticut 06816.

SCHOLASTIC and associated logos are trademarks
and/or registered trademarks of Scholastic Inc.

ISBN 0-439-56312-7

First Scholastic Printing, July 2004

Chapters

Chapter 1
Baseball Fever ....Page 9

Chapter 2
Invisi-boys ....Page 16

Chapter 3
Plan B (or the Naked Truth) ....Page 24

Chapter 4
Play Ball! ....Page 32

Chapter 5
Chaos in the Stands ....Page 40

Chapter 6
Sheen's Lucky Streak ....Page 50

Cindy Vortex sat in class looking smug.
"What's SHE so happy about?" Jimmy
Neutron whispered to his friend Carl
Wheezer. It didn't take long to find out.

"Guess who's going to tonight's game!"
Cindy gloated.

The Retroville Rockets were in the playoffs for the first time ever. Tonight was the final game, and everyone was trying to get tickets.

"Big deal," Jimmy announced. "Sheen will be here with our tickets any minute now."

Just then Sheen ambled into class. "Where are the tickets?" Jimmy asked eagerly.

Sheen looked startled. "Yeah, the tickets . . . " he said.

"Well, the bad news is I never made it to the stadium this weekend to buy the tickets," Sheen admitted.

Jimmy tried not to panic. "Well, is there good news?" he asked.

Sheen grinned. "I watched all 46 hours of the Ultra Lord marathon on TV. It was *awesome!*"

All day, the boys listened to their classmates talking about the game. "We have to go!" Jimmy declared, as they walked home.

"Gosh, Jimmy, I just can't see any way," Carl said sadly.

"Can't see . . . " Jimmy repeated. "BRAIN BLAST! Why didn't I think of that before? Leave everything to me," he continued confidently. "Meet me at the stadium by the outfield fence at six o'clock. We're going to the game!"

A few hours later, Jimmy showed Carl and Sheen his latest invention. "Gentlemen, I give you Invisi-gum!" he said proudly.

"Chew this, and within seconds you will become invisible!"

"Excellent!" Sheen said excitedly. "We'll be like superheroes. Ultra Lord and his trusty sidekick, INVISI-BOY!"

"Um, right," Jimmy replied. "The gum is formulated to last for three hours. That's just long enough to sneak into the stadium, watch the game, and sneak back out!"

"Jimmy," Carl said timidly, "do you know that it only lasts three hours because you've already performed extensive safety testing on it?"

"Well, no," Jimmy admitted. "I didn't have time to test it. But don't worry, guys. It's foolproof!"

Reluctantly, the boys popped the gum in their mouths. A smile spread across Carl's face. "Mmmm, fruity!" he said.

"With subtle hints of cherry and motor oil," Sheen agreed.

Then Sheen looked down at his hands.
"Woo-hooo!" he yelled. "I'm turning invisible!
Look out, evildoers."

Jimmy watched as his own fingers
and hands began to disappear. "Just as I
calculated," he said with a satisfied smile.

"Hello?" Carl called. "Can you guys still
hear me, or am I invisible, too?"

After about a minute, the boys had completely disappeared. But there was one little problem . . .

"Gas planet!" Jimmy moaned. "This formulation only works on organic matter.

It won't have any effect on our clothes."

"Or your hair! I told you not to use so much styling mousse!" Sheen added, pointing.

"The emulsifiers must be preventing optimal absorption," Jimmy muttered. "I see some further development is necessary."

"This is no problem," Jimmy said reassuringly. "We'll just have to take off the stuff that's still visible."

"You mean . . . our clothes?" Carl asked in disbelief.

"You expect us to sneak into a stadium full of people completely naked?" Sheen asked. "This should be an interesting addition to my nightmare repertoire."

"No way, Jimmy!" Carl declared. "No one—not even me—sees me naked!"

"But that's the whole point," Jimmy
explained. "No one will see you. You'll be
totally invisible! We won't even be able to
see ourselves."

The game was about to start, and Jimmy
was determined to see it. "I'll go first," he
said, as he began to peel off his clothes.

After a brief pause, Sheen and then Carl shed their clothes. Now Jimmy, Carl, and Sheen were invisible—or almost.

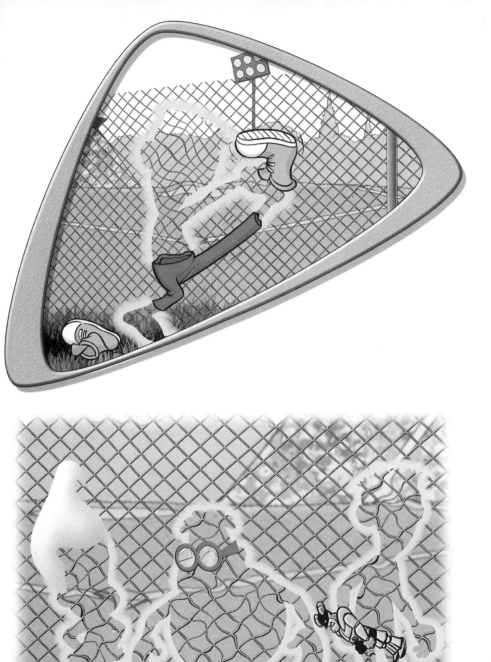

"Great! Now lose the glasses and the
doll, and we can head in," Jimmy told them.

"It's not a doll—it's an *action figure!* And
he goes where I go," Sheen said defiantly.

"And I can't see without my glasses,"
Carl whimpered.

"All right, all right," Jimmy said. "Let's go, men!"

The boys piled up their clothes and wriggled under a bent spot in the fence.

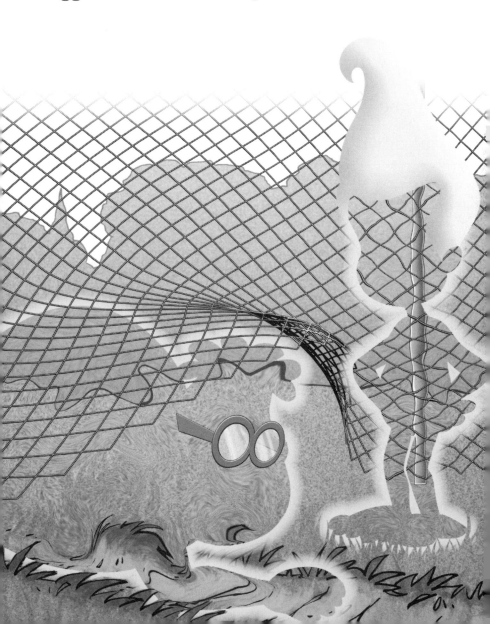

Once they were inside the stadium,
Jimmy looked for a spot in the bleachers.
"Follow me," he instructed quietly. They
climbed a little way up the steps and
sat down.

"Ooh! Chilly!" Carl exclaimed.

"Shhhhh, Carl!" Jimmy whispered. "We can't make any noise!"

"Maybe I'll catch a foul ball," Sheen whispered. "I've always felt destined for fleeting celebrity."

"No, Sheen," Jimmy hissed. "We can't do anything that will call attention to us. We'll be lucky if no one spots my hair, Carl's glasses, or your doll—
I mean action figure."

At that moment Cindy and Libby came walking up the steps. Jimmy watched in disbelief as they took the seats right next to Carl. "Just my luck!" he thought to himself.

The game began, and soon the boys forgot about everything but the action on the field. The Rockets were in top form, but the Comets were just as good. Inning after inning, the score kept tying.

No one noticed the invisible intruders in the stands, and gradually the boys relaxed. They sang "Take Me Out to the Ball Game" with the rest of the crowd. They even did the wave, although no one saw them.

By the top of the ninth inning, Jimmy was feeling very pleased with himself. "Another brilliant invention, Neutron," he thought happily.

Carl leaned over, breaking into Jimmy's

thoughts. "Um, Jimmy, how much longer do you think this game will go?" he whispered.

"I'm not sure, Carl," Jimmy whispered back. "Why?"

"Well, hasn't it been almost three hours?"

Just then a man passed by, holding his little girl's hand. The girl spotted Sheen's Ultra Lord lying on the steps. "Look, Daddy!" she exclaimed. "Someone left their dolly!"

"It's an ac—!" Sheen started to say, but Jimmy clamped an invisible hand over Sheen's invisible mouth.

The little girl reached down. "Don't worry, dolly," she said comfortingly. "You can come home with me."

But as she tried to pick the toy up, it jerked out of her hands. "It's heavy," she said

in surprise. She grabbed the toy again and
gave it a strong pull. But Sheen was holding
on with both hands and pulling back with
all his might.

The little girl set her feet and tried again. Ultra Lord jerked back and forth, up and down, until finally Sheen gave a mighty tug and yanked the toy out of the little girl's

grip. She staggered backward and crashed into a passing peanut vendor. Peanuts and soda flew through the air in a graceful arc, then descended into the stands, directly onto Cindy's head!

"Excellent!" Jimmy thought gleefully, as screams erupted from the stands. Then he noticed the time on the giant scoreboard. "Guys," he hissed to his friends, "I think we'd better blast!"

"But, Jimmy, the game's still tied. And the Rockets are at bat!" Sheen argued.

"Sheen, we're not going to be invisible for much longer," Jimmy said. "I don't know about you, but I'd rather be back in my clothes when I reappear."

The boys quickly began to make their way out of the stands. Jimmy noticed that his fingertips were becoming visible. "Uh-oh, better hurry!" he whispered urgently.

"By my calculations, we have approximately 36.2 seconds before we completely reappear."

Jimmy, Sheen, and Carl ran for the fence and scrambled underneath. With each passing moment, they were becoming more visible. "Grab your clothes!" Jimmy screamed.

The boys had just managed to pull on
their underwear when the final effects of
the Invisi-gum wore off.

"Whew, just in time," Jimmy said, pawing
through the pile of clothing. "Now, where
are my pants?"

Suddenly Jimmy, Carl, and Sheen heard the loud crack of a bat and then an "*Ohhhhh!*" from the stadium. Sheen peered at the field. "The Retroville batter just hit a

long one," he reported. "It's heading right over the fence! They're gonna win the game!"

"The fence?" Carl repeated.

"This fence?" Jimmy asked urgently.

Jimmy turned to see the ball in midair, headed right for them.

"I got it! I got it!" screamed Sheen.

"No, Sheen! Run!" Jimmy yelled. But

it was too late.

As the ball sailed over the fence, Sheen leaped up and caught it. And, to Jimmy and Carl's dismay, the giant screen displayed the whole thing.

There was a gasp from the stands, and then waves of laughter shook the stadium. Jimmy and Carl grabbed the pile of clothes and ran frantically for cover.

Sheen, however, stood and bowed to the crowd. "It was nothing," he said modestly. "Just the fulfillment of a young fan's dreams."

The next morning in school, Libby was waiting for the boys. "So, what did the stadium security officers do to you?" she asked.

"Oh, it was no big deal," Jimmy said. "We just have to scrape all the gum from under

the stadium seats next Saturday."

" . . . And the Saturday after that . . . "
Sheen added.

" . . . And the Saturday after that," Carl
chimed in.

Cindy walked into the room. "Well, if it isn't the Tighty-Whitie Trio!" she said. She held out a newspaper for the class to see. "Has everyone seen this morning's *Retroville Reporter*?"

Carl buried his face in his hands.

"Jimmy, next time we disappear, could we make sure it's permanent?" he groaned.

Libby giggled. "Now, that's what I call a news flash!"

Retroville Reporter

NAKED KIDS NABBED!